SARA TROFA & ELSA KLEVER

TAXI RIDE WITH VICTOR

PRESTEL

Munich · London · New York

VICTOR HAD ALWAYS DREAMED OF BECOMING A TAXI DRIVER. ALERT, FRIENDLY, AND FAST. NO ONE ELSE WOULD KNOW EVERY THE GALAXY'S

GREATEST TAXI DRIVER—
SHORTCUT IN THE GALAXY.

IT'S TRUE THAT VICTOR BECAME A TAXI DRIVER.
IT'S ALSO TRUE HE ALWAYS GOT LOST.
LEFT? RIGHT? TURN HERE? NO – GO STRAIGHT!
A RIDE IN VICTOR'S TAXI WAS SURE
TO BE AN ADVENTURE.

BUT HE ALWAYS TRIED
TO FIND HIS WAY.

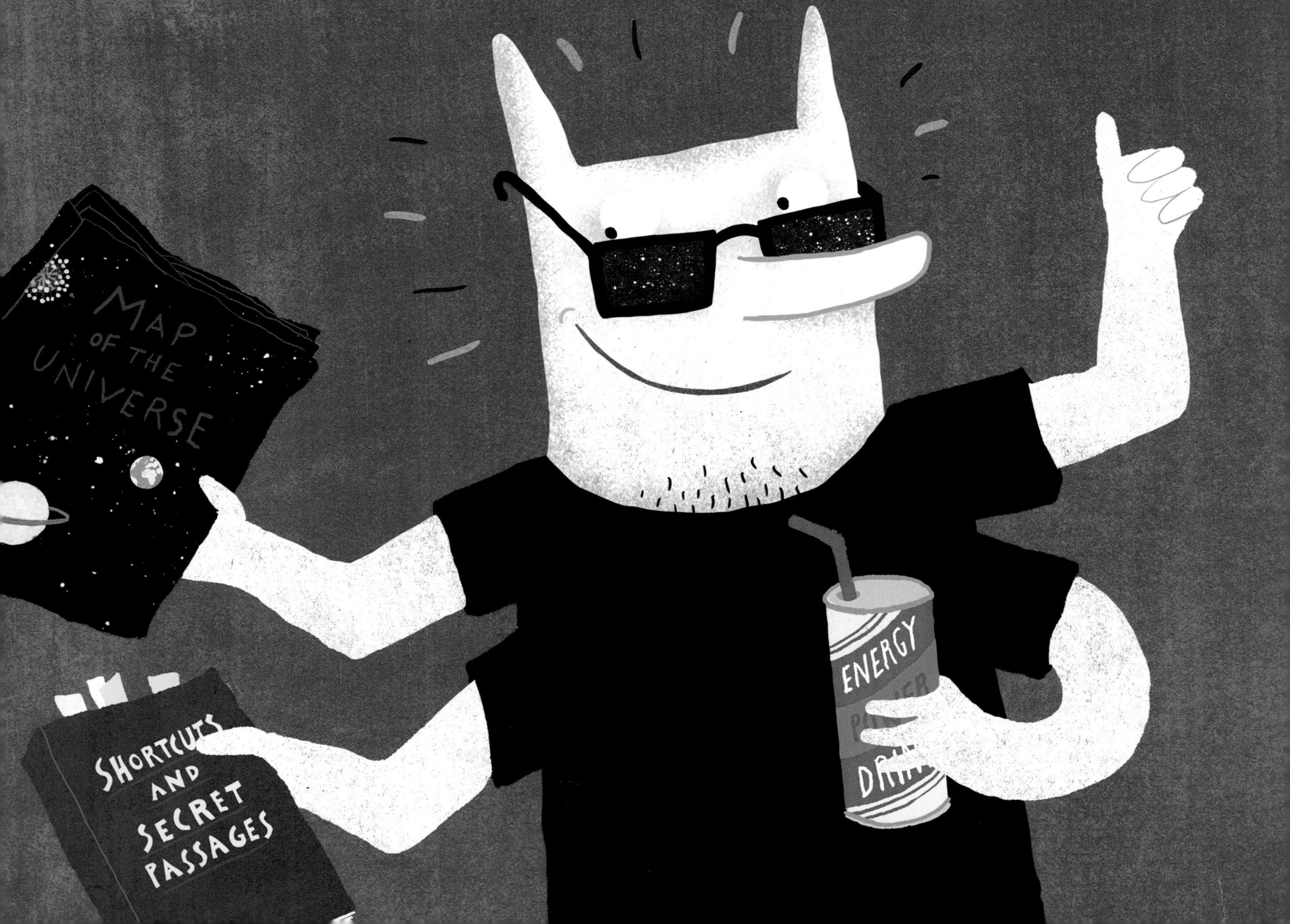

ON MONDAY...

"WHERE TO?"
ASKED VICTOR.

"THE HAIRDRESSER,
PLEASE," REPLIED
A GRAY-HAIRED LADY.

WITH A NOD VICTOR FLEW
STRAIGHT, THEN UP, THEN LEFT...

"ARE YOU SURE THIS IS THE RIGHT WAY?!"

ON TUESDAY...

"WHERE TO?"
ASKED VICTOR.
"LUNA PARK, PLEASE!"
REPLIED A VERY EXCITED BOY.
"MY GRANDMA TOLD ME YOU
TOOK HER THERE
YESTERDAY!"

"I DID?"
MUSED VICTOR,
TURNING RIGHT,
THEN LEFT,
THEN STRAIGHT
AHEAD...

ON WEDNESDAY...

"WHERE TO?"
ASKED VICTOR.
"THE CENTRAL LIBRARY!
HURRY, PLEASE,
I'M LATE FOR WORK!"
REPLIED THE HEAD
LIBRARIAN, GOBBLING
HIS BREAKFAST IN
THE BACK OF
THE CAB.
"AND MAKE SURE
YOU TAKE THE RIGHT
ROUTE. I'VE HEARD
YOU'VE BEEN QUITE
DISTRACTED
LATELY..."

OFF VICTOR FLEW,
FIRST LEFT,
THEN RIGHT,
THEN STRAIGHT AHEAD
BEFORE TAKING ANOTHER LEFT...

ON THURSDAY...

"WHERE TO?"
ASKED VICTOR,
WHO WAS ANXIOUS
NOT TO TAKE
ANOTHER
WRONG TURN.

TAXI

"THE DENTIST,
PLEASE!" REPLIED
A WAILING GHOST.
"YOU MIGHT HAVE NOTICED
THAT I HAVE NO TEETH!"

VICTOR ACCELERATED STRAIGHT,
THEN LEFT, THEN RIGHT,
THEN RIGHT AGAIN...

UNTIL THE
GHOST FOUND
ITSELF
AT THE
MAD
SCIENTIST'S
FUNHOUSE
LABORATORY.

ON FRIDAY...

"WHERE TO?" ASKED VICTOR.
"THE FLORIST!" SANG THE MAD SCIENTIST.
"I'M GOING TO BUY SOME FLOWERS FOR MY
NEW FRIEND, THE GHOST!"
"UH-OH," WONDERED VICTOR.
"DID I MAKE ANOTHER
WRONG TURN?"

AND LEFT HE WENT,
THEN STRAIGHT,
THEN UP, AND
UP AGAIN...

ON SATURDAY...

"WHERE TO?" ASKED VICTOR.
"THE TOP OF THE HIGHEST MOUNTAIN, PLEASE!" REPLIED A DARK AND HEAVY CLOUD,
HOPING TO DELIVER A DRAMATIC THUNDERSTORM AT ITS PEAK.
WORRIED IT WOULD RAIN INSIDE HIS CAB, VICTOR DROVE VERY FAST...
STRAIGHT, RIGHT, DOWN, LEFT, UP AND THROUGH...
UNTIL HE REACHED A PLANET HE HAD NEVER BEEN TO.

IT WAS THE
DRIEST REALM
HE HAD EVER SEEN.

BUT THE CLOUD,
WHO WAS BURSTING
AT THE SEAMS,
GOT OFF JUST IN
TIME TO RAIN,
RAIN,
RAIN!

ON SUNDAY...

"WHERE TO?"
ASKED VICTOR.
"TAKE ME BACK TO
MY RAINLESS
REALM **NOW!**"
DEMANDED A QUEEN
WHO HAD LOST
HER WAY.

"I'M ON IT," SAID VICTOR
WITH CONFIDENCE.
STRAIGHT AHEAD, BETWEEN
AND LEFT, THEN RIGHT HE SPED...

EVERY DAY OF THE WEEK, NO MATTER HOW
CONFIDENT HE FELT, VICTOR ALWAYS GOT LOST.
HE LOOKED SO FRUSTRATED!
BUT THERE I WAS, SITTING IN HIS CAB,
READY TO TAKE HIM TO A VERY SPECIAL PLACE.

"WHERE TO?"
HE ASKED WITH A SMILE.
"THE POST OFFICE,
PLEASE," I REPLIED.

AND DOWN HE WENT,
THEN UP AND RIGHT,
THEN LEFT...

HE CERTAINLY
WASN'T GOING
THE RIGHT
WAY...

PARKING

S
SUPERMARKET
S
S

"UM, DID I SAY
POST OFFICE?
I'M SORRY,
I MEANT THE GYM!"

STILL SMILING,
VICTOR LOOPED
AROUND,
WENT STRAIGHT,
THEN LEFT,
THEN STRAIGHT,
AGAIN ...

"WHUPS!
DID I SAY GYM?
SILLY ME,
I MEANT
THE BAKERY!"

AND THAT WAS OUR RIDE. VICTOR TOOK SO MANY WRONG TURNS HE FINALLY FOUND HIMSELF RIGHT IN THE MIDDLE OF...

A BIG SURPRISE PARTY
FOR VICTOR, WHO
HAD BROUGHT US ALL
SUCH UNEXPECTED
HAPPINESS.
IT WAS GRANDMA'S IDEA,
HER GRANDSON WHO
SPREAD THE WORD,
THE LIBRARIAN
WHO WROTE
THE INVITATIONS,
THE GHOST WHO PUT UP
THE DECORATIONS
(AND MADE THE PLAYLIST),
THE MAD SCIENTIST
WHO BAKED THE CAKE,
AND I, WELL...
I BROUGHT VICTOR!

WE ALL HAD
FANCY HAIRDOS, STYLED BY THE LOST QUEEN,
WHO HAD FOUND HER TRUE SELF AS QUEEN OF THE BEAUTY SALON!

THE PEOPLE FROM THE DRIEST REALM COULDN'T
COME TO THE PARTY, BUT THEY SENT
A LETTER:

To VICTOR,
the galaxy's greatest
taxi driver,
Thank you for bringing us
so much rain!
We are soaked
with happiness!

PS: That really was the best
rainstorm I could possibly
rain. Love,
cloudy cloud

AND THAT'S HOW VICTOR REALIZED HE WAS
A NATURAL, MAYBE NOT AT DRIVING TAXIS, BUT
AT BRINGING PEOPLE HAPPINESS!

SARA TROFA was born in Montferrat, Italy. She is a teacher and an author. Her first book was published in France in 2015.

ELSA KLEVER is an acclaimed illustrator whose artwork has appeared in numerous publications. She was the winner of the 2015 Austrian Children's Book Award. She lives in Hamburg, Germany.

TAXI RIDE WITH VICTOR was shortlisted for the World Illustration Awards 2018.

© Text by Sara Trofa
© Illustrations by Elsa Klever
An adaption of the original German edition published under the title:
Taxifahrt mit Victor
© Tulipan Verlag GmbH München / Germany, 2018
www.tulipan-verlag.de
© for the English edition: 2019,
Prestel Verlag, Munich · London · New York
A member of Verlagsgruppe Random House GmbH
Neumarkter Strasse 28 · 81673 Munich

Prestel Publishing Ltd.
14-17 Wells Street
London W1T 3PD

Prestel Publishing
900 Broadway, Suite 603
New York, NY 10003

In respect to links in the book, the Publisher expressly notes that no illegal content was discernible on the linked sites at the time the links were created. The Publisher has no influence at all over the current and future design, content or authorship of the linked sites. For this reason the Publisher expressly disassociates itself from all content on linked sites that has been altered since the link was created and assumes no liability for such content.

Library of Congress Control Number: 2018965323
A CIP catalogue record for this book is available from the British Library.

Copyediting: John Son
Project management: Melanie Schöni
Production management: Susanne Hermann
Printing and binding: DZS Grafik

MIX
Paper from
responsible sources
FSC® C106600

Verlagsgruppe Random House FSC® N001967

Printed in Slovenia

ISBN 978-3-7913-7406-2
www.prestel.com